# SARAI

## SAVES THE MUSIC

## SARAI GONZALEZ
## AND
## MONICA BROWN

SCHOLASTIC INC.

30922 9928

Text copyright © 2019 by Sarai Gonzalez
Illustrations by Christine Almeda copyright © 2019 by Scholastic Inc.

ISBN 978-1-338-26094-6

10 9 8 7 6 5 4 3 2 1        19 20 21 22 23

Printed in the U.S.A.        40

First printing 2019

Book design by Carolyn Bull

To my little sisters, Josephine and Lucia, for always cheering me on. I love you so much. And to my AWESOME parents for always being there for me and telling me there's nothing I can't do. I love you.
—SG

To Brent, with gratitude.
—MB

# CONTENTS

# RISE AND SPARKLE

"Good morning, world! It's going to be an awesome day!" I say, but not too loud. The rest of my family is asleep. I look through my closet, and it's all glitter and sequins and sparkles. *Not that*, I think as I take out my favorite jean jacket. *More sparkles!* I put on my sparkle tights, denim skirt, and a white T-shirt that has a glittery cupcake on it. I've always liked sparkly things, but ever since I discovered Stefanie "Sparkles" Sanchez, I LOVE them. Sparkles Sanchez is a singer, dancer, and

entertainer, and when I grow up, I want to be just like her! She's Latina, like me, and she's from the Bronx, which isn't that far from here. She sings the best songs EVER—all about girl power—and glitter. Her songs have names like "You Are a Shooting Star," "Glitter and Gleam," and "Shimmer and Shake." They always make me feel like dancing, and dancing makes me happy. My cousin JuJu and I are part of the Playful Primas, a dance group, and I'm into music too. I'm also part of the Super Awesome Sister-Cousin Fun Club, which I started myself. I like the feeling that comes from belonging to things!

I'm a member of the school band at Martin Luther King Jr. Elementary, and Ms. Cruz says I have lots of potential! I play the snare drum. I love the sound the drum makes when I tap my drumsticks—it reminds me of the heels of a flamenco dancer and lightning cracks and movie music and marches. When I use my special brush on the drum, it's quieter, but it makes it seem like something exciting is about to happen. I wonder what exciting thing is going to happen today?

# CHAPTER 1

# FEEL THE MUSIC

My sister Lucía and I take the bus to school, and as soon as we get on, she's immediately surrounded by kids.

"What's up, Lucía?" someone says.

"How are you, LuLu?" someone else jokes, using Lucía's nickname.

"I am so fabulous!" LuLu says, smiling. "It's going to be a fun day!" Everyone loves Lucía, and she has lots of friends. I have plenty of people who love me, but most of them aren't at Martin

Luther King Jr. Elementary. Luckily, a few are, like my favorite librarian, Ms. Milligan; my band teacher, Ms. Cruz; and my new best friend, Christina. I have an old best friend, Isa Lopez, but she moved to Washington, D.C., last month. I was really sad at first, but then I met Christina McKay, and I felt a whole lot better. Christina is quiet and spends a lot of time writing in her journal, but she's really fun too. Isa and I are now best pen-pal friends. It's fun having a pen pal—it's kind of like writing in a diary, except that you know someone else will read it!

"Hi, Christina!" I say when she gets on the bus. She's easy to find, even though she usually wears dark clothes. I just look for curly bright-red hair, and there she is. "How's it going?"

"Good," Christina says. "I finished two whole chapters last night."

"Congratulations," I say, smiling. "What were they about?" Christina is writing an EPIC adventure called *The Unicorn Tales* about magical kingdoms and fantasy places. She wants to be a writer when she grows up. Christina explained to me that an epic story is an especially long one that stars a hero, or, in the case of her story, a heroine. I like the idea of a special girl saving the day!

Christina plays the triangle in our band, which is perfect for her because she's really precise and has a delicate touch. I like to bang things.

Once, Valéria teased Christina, saying, "You got the easy one."

Valéria thinks she's extra special just because she plays the flute. "The triangle's not even a real instrument!" she told Christina.

But unfortunately for Valéria, Ms. Cruz overheard.

"The triangle is a beautiful and complex instrument," Ms. Cruz explained. "It's used in classical music, folk music, and even rock music. Mozart, Liszt, and Beethoven used it, and we will too!" Valéria was quiet after that, which was nice. I don't know why she likes to tease me and whoever I'm friends with, but Christina has a few ideas.

"She's just jealous of you," she told me one day, after Valéria rolled her eyes at something I said.

"Jealous?" I said. "Why?"

"Because you're so smart, and because you're you!" Christina said, smiling.

It's nice to have a friend like Christina.

We have music class after lunch three times a week. The other two days we go to the library. While we wait for class to start, it's usually pretty loud because it takes a little bit of time to settle down after recess. We are supposed to warm up, but we also play around, talk, and have fun. Auggie is the lead percussionist, and he has a whole drum kit with lots of different drums. I'm on the snare drum, along with a couple of others, and a girl named Ellie plays the bass drum. I like watching Ellie play because she sort of dances when she plays. Christina is with our group because the triangle is in the percussion family too.

Valéria and her best friend, Kayla, are in the woodwind section with the flutes and clarinets.

Our school starts Beginning Band in third grade. This is our second year as a class, which means we get to participate in the school concert for the first time! As soon as Ms. Cruz walks in, we settle down fast. She's a little intimidating, but she inspires us too. We always start by practicing scales, but once we are working on songs, she says things like, "Feel the music!" and "Music is a universal language!" She also has a bunch of shirts with funny pictures and sayings. One says "Band Geek" and another has a picture of a cat playing the drums. Most teachers don't wear T-shirts, but I think that Ms. Cruz gets to do whatever she wants because she once said, "I'm a creative."

"How can you be *a* creative?" I asked her. "You *are* creative. Not *a* creative!" I said, remembering my grammar lessons.

"I tend to get *creative* with grammar, that's why!" Ms. Cruz laughed.

"Then I want to be *a* creative too," I said. "I sing and dance and play the drums! And Christina writes too—that's really creative!"

"We're ALL creatives!" Ms. Cruz said. "Now let's make some music!" That was one of the best music classes ever.

Today, Ms. Cruz wants to get down to business. "Attention, students!" Ms. Cruz says. "We need to really focus today because our big performance is in two weeks. Your two main songs are sounding so good that I have a surprise for you."

"I love surprises!" I say.

"So do I, which is why I didn't tell you about this before," says Ms. Cruz. "I think we have time to work on one more song for the show. How

would you feel about a contemporary pop song?"
she asks. The whole class cheers.

"What song?" asks Auggie.

"I have some ideas!" says Kayla.

"Me too!" I say.

"Since we want our concert to be spectacular,
I figured we needed some spectacular sparks.
With that in mind, I've chosen a song I hope you'll
like," Ms. Cruz says, looking around the room,
smiling. "We're going to perform 'Glitter and
Gleam' by Sparkles Sanchez."

"Yay!" the class cheers. For once, we all agree on something. Sparkles Sanchez is the most awesome singer ever, and now I'm going to learn to play one of her songs and not just any song—her number-one hit.

"Percussionists, I'm going to rely on you for leadership because this is a drum-heavy piece. In fact, there are two drum solos, which I'll assign later on. For now, let's learn this new piece of music," Ms. Cruz says as she passes around some sheet music. I'm so excited I accidentally knock over my music stand. I hear Valéria and Kayla snicker, but I don't even care. I'm going to learn a Sparkles Sanchez song!

# CHAPTER 2

## GARAGE CHAT

I don't have a snare drum to practice on at home, but I DO have a drum pad and I practice as often as I can, especially when I have time, like today. I love Saturdays. It's the one day of the week that our family has nothing officially planned, and we can just have fun together. I really hope that Ms. Cruz chooses me for the drum solo. I imagine myself up onstage, with a spotlight shining on my hair. It's extra shiny because I've sprayed it with glitter sparkles . . .

"Sarai!" Lucía says. "You're daydreaming again! Josie and I want to have a meeting of the Super Awesome Sister-Cousin Fun Club. Are you in?"

"Let's invite the Js," Josie signs. The Js are our cousins JuJu, who is my age, and the twins, Javier and Jade, who are younger. Ever since they moved in a couple of blocks away, we've gotten to see them more often, and we already saw them a lot.

"That's a great idea, Josie!" I sign back to her. "Mom, can we see the Js?"

"I'll call your Tía Sofía and ask if the kids can come over," Mom says. The Js live in a big house with my Tata, my Mama Rosí, and my Tío Miguel.

"That sounds awesome," I say, and pretty soon I hear Mom talking on the phone to her sister, my Tía Sofía. Then I hear her talking to her mom, my Mama Rosí.

"Change of plans," she says when she hangs up. "We are ALL invited over to the Js' house this afternoon, and Tía Sofía made me promise that we'd stay for dinner. She and Mama Rosí are making ceviche."

"Yum!" Josie signs. "I love ceviche!" I love it too. It's whitefish in lime juice. It has red onions and cilantro, and we usually eat it with sweet potatoes and corn.

"Family fiesta!" Lucía says. "Let's party!"

We walk the short distance to the Js' house, passing the Martínez and Sons market on the corner.

"Let's stop so I can pick up some avocados," Mom says. Mr. Martínez is sweeping the sidewalk in front of the store.

"¡Buenas tardes!" he says.

"Good afternoon, Señor Martínez!" I answer back. We talk for a little bit, Mom picks up a few things, and then we are on our way. Down the block, we walk past Señora Sanchez, who is out tending her flowers.

"Your flowers are the prettiest in the neighborhood, Señora Sanchez!" I say.

"Well, let me cut you some, sweetie!" she says. "You must be on your way to your grandmother's house. You can bring her some flowers."

I thank her with a hug, and promise to bring by some cupcakes the next time I make them because everyone knows that Señora Sanchez has a sweet tooth.

When we finally get to my grandparents' house, I ring the doorbell, even though I know I can just walk in if I want to. Mama Rosí answers the door at her house, and I say, "Surprise!" and hand her the beautiful bouquet of flowers. "These are from Señora Sanchez."

"She is the loveliest woman," Mama Rosí says, taking the flowers and putting them in a vase. "They smell wonderful. I'm going to invite Señora Sanchez over to lunch next week."

Javier and Jade run down the stairs, jumping the last two, and JuJu comes out of her room and gives me a hug. JuJu is one of my best friends.

"Happy Saturday!" she says. "I'm so glad you are here."

Lucía, one of the co-presidents of the Super Awesome Sister-Cousin Fun Club, decides to call the meeting to order. "Let's start the meeting," she says.

The Js have a big picnic table that can fit all of us at once. When we are all sitting, Tata brings out a pitcher of chicha morada and some cups.

"Yum!" I say. I love the Peruvian drink made with purple corn, sugar, spices, and pineapple.

"Any new business?" JuJu asks.

"Yes!" I say, raising my hand. Josie points to me. She's a co-president of the Super Awesome Sister-Cousin Fun Club too. Actually, every member is a co-president because that's the only way we could agree to have the club in the first place. I look at my sisters and cousins.

"I need a super awesome brainstorming session."

"Okay," JuJu says. "What about?"

"Well, my baking career is really taking off with Sarai's Sweets, but if I'm going to be a singer, dancer, talk show host, and entertainer like Sparkles Sanchez, I need to get going.

So I've decided on a new project, called *Sarai's Garage Chat*."

"But garages don't talk!" Javier says.

"Of course not," I say, "but I do! And the only space I have for my TV studio is the garage. Dad said he'd move the car on filming days. I'm going to put my desk and few chairs there and interview people. Tata is going to tape the episodes on his phone."

"So what do you need our help for?" Lucía asks. "This club is about all of us, not just you."

"I want to interview each of you!" I say. "I thought I could start with Javier and Jade and ask what it's like to be twins."

"But I don't know what it's like to not be a twin, so how can I know what's different about being a twin?" Jade asks.

"Why don't you interview me?" Lucía says.

"On what subject?" I ask.

"We can talk about how fabulous I am!" Lucía says, laughing.

"Hmmmmm," I say.

"The Playful Primas can perform!" JuJu says.

"But how can I interview myself?" I say. "Maybe you can dance a solo, JuJu."

"But one prima alone isn't exactly playful," she says. "Let me think about it."

"Any more discussion?" Josie signs.

"I think you need to do a little more research if you are going to film a talk show," JuJu advises. "You need a theme for each show."

"You mean like a main idea?" I say, thinking of my reading lessons at school.

"Yes!" JuJu says.

"Next order of business!" JuJu signs and says. "What do you want to do today?"

"Let's convince our parents to let us have a sleepover!" Lucía says, and we all agree.

# CHAPTER 3

# BAD NEWS

When Ms. Cruz walks into our music classroom on Monday, I can tell something is wrong. For one thing, she isn't smiling. And for another, she's wearing a suit! I've never seen her in one, and I hardly recognize her. Then I notice that she's wearing a T-shirt that says "Music Is Magic" under her blazer, and I smile to myself.

"Good afternoon, students," she says, without her usual smile. Auggie raises his hand.

"Ms. Cruz," he says, "is something wrong?"

"Well," she says, "I have some bad news. I just came from a meeting at the school district offices. They're cutting budgets across the county, and they've decided to cut the funds from the elementary music programs."

"No way!" I say.

"That's not fair!" says Auggie. Everyone in the class starts talking at once.

"What does that mean for us?" Valéria asks. "Will we still get to do our show?"

"What does it mean for you?" I ask Ms. Cruz. "Will you lose your job?" Ms. Cruz has tears in her eyes. I've never seen a teacher cry before, and I feel worried.

"Don't worry about me. The show must go on, or in our case, the concert. I want us to go out with a bang!" Ms. Cruz says, lifting up her chin.

"I have a question," I say, raising my hand. "Isn't there anything we can do? Fundraise? Protest? Sign petitions?" Ms. Cruz looks at me and smiles for the first time.

"Thanks for your suggestions, Sarai. The answer is . . . maybe." *"Maybe" isn't a real answer,* I think to myself. It's usually what adults say when they really mean no but don't want to tell you that. But Ms. Cruz isn't done.

"I'm going to try and get on the agenda for this month's PTA meeting," she says.

"I can help with that!" I say. "I know the president of the Parent-Teacher Association!" He happens to be my dad, Juan Carlos Gonzalez.

My dad is super involved with our school, and also Josie's school for deaf and hearing-impaired children. Ever since Josie was born with a heart condition, my dad has stayed at home with her and us. My mom works outside the house for a hospital. My sister Josie has had lots of struggles with her health, but she never gives up, and neither do we. We are the Gonzalez family five and we fight for what we believe in! Right now, I believe that our music program is worth fighting for.

"You'll see," I tell Ms. Cruz. "Everything is going to be all right. The PTA won't let us down."

"Okay, Sarai," Ms. Cruz says, "I'll talk to your father about getting on the agenda, and I'll see what I can do. We should ALL be thinking about what we can do because this music program belongs to each and every one of us!"

"I agree!" says Auggie.

"Me too," says Christina.

"Thanks for your enthusiasm, students." Ms. Cruz says. "Let's feel the beat of the music, my charming creatives!" *Now she sounds like the Ms. Cruz I'm used to,* I think, and I'm relieved.

After school, I can't stop fidgeting. I walk back and forth in our family room and can't sit still long enough to work on my homework.

"What's wrong, mi estrella?" Tata asks me. My grandpa watches my sister and me after school every day until my father gets home with Josie. I love that he's always waiting on the porch when we get off the bus. I also love that he calls me his estrella, his star, but today I can't think about anything except our music program.

"*When* are Dad and Josie going to get home?" I say. "It's almost five o'clock! Can I call him?"

"Sarai, Josie had speech therapy after school today, and you know your dad and Josie have a long drive home. We don't call anyone who's driving unless it's an emergency."

*It is an emergency*, I think. But I've explained the situation to Tata, and he doesn't seem too worried.

"It will all work out," he promises.

"It will!" says Lucía confidently. She likes Ms. Cruz too, even though she hasn't had her as a teacher yet. I told Ms. Cruz about how Lucía is obsessed with Hawaii, and the next day Ms. Cruz brought in a ukulele, an instrument that looked like a little guitar. I brought Lucía into the music room at recess, and Ms. Cruz explained that the ukulele originated in Hawaii in the nineteenth century, inspired by instruments brought by Portuguese immigrants. Then she played a Hawaiian song for Lucía, who was so excited she could hardly talk.

*Finally*, I hear the minivan in the driveway. I meet Dad and Josie at the door.

"Dad!" I say. "I need your help!"

"Are you sure you don't need your mom's help?" he says, joking. "Because she'll be home any minute."

"No, I need *your* help because you are the PTA president," I say, and then I explain to him what's going on with the music program. Dad frowns when I tell him, which isn't a good sign.

"Sarai," he says, "our PTA struggles to fund the programs we already sponsor. You know the students at our school don't come from wealthy families."

"You can fundraise!" I say.

"But there's a limit to how much struggling families can donate," Dad explains.

"Then let's do a petition! That doesn't cost anything. Or a letter writing campaign," I say.

"That's an interesting idea," Dad says.

"Can you at least put Ms. Cruz on the agenda? She's one of the best teachers I've ever had, and she might lose her job!"

"That, I can do," Dad says. "I'll email her first thing tomorrow morning."

"Okay," I say. "Can I come to the meeting?"

"It's called the Parent-Teacher Association, not the Parent-Teacher-Student Association," Dad says.

"Then you don't mind if I do my own thing?" I ask Dad.

"I'm almost afraid to ask what 'doing your own thing' means," Dad says.

To be honest, I'm not sure what "my own thing" means just yet, but I will! I just need a plan.

# CHAPTER 4

# GLITTER AND GLEAM

"Thanks for helping me get on the PTA agenda, Sarai," Ms. Cruz tells me at the beginning of class the next day.

"You're welcome," I say. "I have an idea about saving our music program. Can I share it with the class?"

"Sure," says Ms. Cruz.

"I think we should invite everyone in the neighborhood to our concert and make it a fundraiser!"

"Yeah!" Auggie says. "Make everyone pay."

"We don't want to prevent anyone from attending," Ms. Cruz says. "I think we should make donations optional and separate so no one is embarrassed if they don't have any extra money to contribute."

"The mayor has a hotline!" Auggie says. "We should all leave messages for her."

"Great idea!" Ellie says, snapping her fingers. "I like it!"

"Should we start our calling and letter writing now?" I ask Ms. Cruz.

"I love everyone's ideas, but I think we should use this time to focus on music."

"Okay," I say, and turn to my music. It's hard to concentrate with so much going on. I'm already thinking about what I'll write in my letter to the editor. I miss so many notes that Ms. Cruz says, "Focus your attention, Sarai." But my attention is wandering every which way.

When Lucía and I get home from school, Tata is sitting on the porch, smiling.

"Something arrived for you in the mail!" he says. "It's on the kitchen table."

"It's here! It's here!" I yell, and Lucía and Tata come running in. "My poster has arrived! Everyone, come see!" Lucía and Josie come over to where I'm sitting at the table, carefully opening up my special gift. I ordered the poster almost two months ago. I slide the poster out carefully. There she is—my musical idol. Stefanie "Sparkles" Sanchez—singer, dancer, entertainer. All the things I want to be when I grow up, and more.

*"Don't be afraid to shine!"* is written at the

bottom of the poster, with Sparkles Sanchez's signature below. In the picture, Sparkles is holding a microphone, wearing a purple tutu, pink high-tops, and a black leather jacket, which has the word "Sparkles" spelled out in pink sequins. Sparkles has long black hair with the one strip in front that is dyed magenta.

"Wow," Lucía says.

"Wow," I say back. "Do you think Mom would let me dye a strip of my hair pink?"

"No!" says Tata, shaking his head. "Don't even ask."

I put the new poster up in my room over my bed. I pick up a pen and pretend it's a microphone. I think about how much fun it will be to perform the Sparkles Sanchez song at the concert. But then I start to feel a little sad. By this time next year, we might not even have a music program at Martin Luther King Jr. Elementary. I wonder what Sparkles Sanchez would do in this situation. Then I think of the lyrics to her song "Glitter and Gleam":

When the lights go out
And all seems dark,
Look within
And find the spark.
Your best self
Will glitter and gleam.
You are strong.
I'm on your team.

Glitter, glitter,
Glitter, and gleam.

Shine bright,
Reflect the light.

Glitter, glitter,
Glitter, and gleam.

That's it! I've got it! I've found my spark! We are Team Martin Luther King Jr. Elementary, and we are not giving up our music program without a fight! I have an idea that's worth trying. I'm going to need Tata's help, but he's never let me down.

At school the next day, I tell Christina and Auggie my plan, and they agree that it's a good one. But we need all, or at least most, of the kids in our music class to make it happen. We divide up the class and agree to talk to everyone at lunch. Auggie is going to talk with Ms. Cruz. Valéria and Kayla are surprised when Christina and I walk over to them in the cafeteria.

"Hi," I say to them. "How are you?" They just

Hi...

look at me. "I want to talk to you about something important."

"So talk," Valéria says with a shrug.

"Well, you may not know this, but I'm starting a talk show called *Sarai's Garage Chat*, which will film in my garage—" I explain, and Kayla cuts me off.

"That's weird," she says. "Who ever heard of a talk show that films in a garage?"

"Well, weird or not, I want to tell you my idea about saving the music program," I say, getting frustrated.

"You do want to save the program, right?" Christina asks in her quiet, serious voice.

"Of course," Valéria says. "I love playing the flute. What's your idea?"

"Well, this Saturday I thought we could film a special episode of my show and talk about the music program at Martin Luther King Jr. Elementary. If we have enough people from class, we can play our cover of Sparkles Sanchez's song 'Glitter and Gleam.' Then we can upload the video and share it, inviting the community to come to our concert and donate money for the music program."

"Like a public service announcement?" asks Kayla.

"Yes!" I say.

"Your parents don't mind having the whole class in their garage Saturday?" Valéria asks. "Mine sure would."

"Not at all," I answer, "but they did say that they will need to get permission from everyone's parents before we film. Let me know if you can come."

I hand each of them a piece of paper with my address and my parents' names and phone number on it.

"You know, this isn't a bad idea," Valéria says, surprising me. "That could actually be pretty cool."

I don't see Auggie the rest of lunch, but after school at the bus stop, he runs up to me and says, "Guess what?"

"What?" I ask.

"Almost everyone can come!" Auggie says. "And that includes Ms. Cruz! She's going to bring the instruments!"

"That's awesome," I tell Auggie. "We've got this."

"Yes, we do," he agrees, giving me a high five. I knew Auggie was a good drummer, but I never realized that he's a good friend too.

# CHAPTER 5

# GLITTER GIRLS

On Friday night, JuJu comes over to help me plan the first-ever episode of *Sarai's Garage Chat*. We've decided that JuJu will be the producer and Tata the director. I will be the star interviewer, of course.

"What about me?" Josie signs.

"And me?" Lucía says, stomping her foot. "I want to be on the show too!"

"You can be," says JuJu. "Let me think . . ."

"I know!" I say. "You can be the . . . Glitter Girls!"

"*Sarai's Garage Chat*, featuring the Glitter Girls," says JuJu. "I like the sound of that."

"Me too!" Josie signs.

"Me three!" Lucía says, and disappears into her room. Josie follows her. We ask Dad to help us move my desk into the garage, along with a couple of table chairs. Tata is already setting up his camera phone on a tripod.

"Where did you get that, Tata?" I ask. "It looks so professional!"

"I found it at a garage sale," he says. My Tata loves garage sales almost as much as he loves gadgets. "This way I can zoom in and out without the camera moving and the picture will be steady. Get behind the desk, Sarai, so I can see what this will look like. Sit next to her, JuJu."

We try different camera positions and then figure out where the camera will be when we have the whole garage full of students.

"So first, I'll introduce myself; then we'll talk about why music programs are important, and then we'll perform," I say.

"We need to make cue cards with individual lines on them," says JuJu, thinking out loud. "That way, no one will forget their lines." All of a sudden, there's a commotion. Josie and Lucía run into the garage, all dressed up in scarves and old Halloween costumes, and they have their fists full of something.

"We're the Glitter Girls!" Lucía yells. "And we're here to start the show!" Then she and Josie

run toward us and throw open their hands, which are full of glitter. The glitter gets in my eyes, and JuJu's too.

"CUT!" yells Tata, and he stops filming. He takes us inside, and Mom rinses out our eyes with water. When we come out of the bathroom, Mom says that we should probably throw something other than glitter.

"But we're the Glitter Girls!" Lucía says.

"We sparkle!" Josie signs and says.

"I have an idea," Tata says, looking at Josie's and Lucía's disappointed faces. "How about if you two are the Confetti Girls?"

"Where are we going to get confetti?" Josie signs and says.

"We'll make it ourselves," I say. "We can use the sparkly wrapping paper Mom has."

"Great idea!" says JuJu. "You two can still be the Glitter Girls because you will still sparkle."

"Where are the scissors?" asks Lucía.

"Why don't we let JuJu and Sarai do the cutting," Mom says.

"We've had enough injuries for one night," Dad agrees. "Josie, Lucía, let's get ready for bed."

# CHAPTER 6

# READY, SET, ACTION!

The sun is shining when kids start showing up at our house on Saturday morning. The garage looks great, and Tata has the camera set up in the driveway, ready to film. JuJu and I made him a megaphone out of construction paper that says "*El Director*." Then we made one for JuJu that reads "*The Boss*."

Mom and Dad are outside, talking to the parents and inviting them to stay and watch. Ms. Cruz helps us get the instruments ready, and

JuJu explains how everything will work. She has a clipboard and looks very professional. She's even marked places for kids to stand with masking tape on the floor of the garage. Finally, it's time.

"Ready, set, action!" Tata says into his megaphone, and he starts filming.

"Welcome to the first-ever episode of *Sarai's Garage Chat* with your host, me, Sarai Gonzalez, and featuring . . . the Glitter Girls!" I say, and on cue, Josie and Lucía run across the stage throwing handfuls of confetti in the air. They are dressed in matching tutus with their hair in pigtails with ribbons.

"We are filming a special episode today because frankly, people, we have a crisis," I say, looking straight into the camera. "Our school district, right here in New Jersey, is about to cut funding to all our elementary music programs. I've invited several of our school band members here to explain why that's not a good idea. Let's start with our star drummer, Auggie."

"Let me throw some facts at you," Auggie says, tapping his cymbals to make his point. "Students who study music do better in math, reading, and writing than those who don't study music!"

"Let's hear from our clarinet player, Kayla. What are your thoughts?" I ask.

"Kids involved with the arts are less likely to drop out of school!" she says, reading from the cue card Javier is holding up.

"Let's ask our bass drummer what she thinks," I say. "Ellie?"

"Kids who play musical instruments have higher self-esteem than those who don't!" Ellie says, and then spins around in a circle, ending with a few taps on her drum. She's got a lot of flair.

"Wow," I say, "I think the evidence is in. School music programs are important! That's why we are asking everyone watching to come to our concert on Friday in the Martin Luther King Jr. gym. Donate if you can, or just come and enjoy and write a letter to the district in support of school music programs. And we are going to give you a preview of one of the songs we are going to perform, 'Glitter and Gleam' by Sparkles Sanchez! Did you know that she participated in school music programs in the Bronx when she was growing up?" I turn to Valéria.

"You never know who the next musical superstar will be," Valéria says, going off script and flipping her hair, "so support music education in all our schools."

"Thanks, Valéria," I say. "And at our school, EVERYONE is a star. And now it's time for our cover song. Ready? Hit it!"

We sound great! We do our big finish and end with the drums pounding, the cymbals smashing, and everyone cheering. I look straight at the camera and say, "Thank you for watching this episode of *Sarai's Garage Chat*! Remember, music is for everyone. Support music in New Jersey schools!"

And then Lucía and Josie run toward the camera and throw sparkly confetti at it.

"Cut!" says Tata. "That's a wrap." He sounds like a real director. We all cheer, and Ms. Cruz cheers the loudest. Valéria even compliments Josie and Lucía on their Glitter Girl costumes. I can hardly believe it.

"That was AMAZING!" Ms. Cruz says. "Your best performance yet!"

My parents make sure we have everyone's parents' permission to post the video online, the kids in my class leave, and then Tata, JuJu, and

I spend the rest of the day editing it to look really cool. We even have a link to our school's fund-raising page. It takes a long time, and Mom and Dad insist we take a break for dinner. Later on, Mama Rosí calls and asks where Tata is. He gets on the phone to say, "Hola, amor, I'll be home in an hour. I'm helping our granddaughter save the world again." After he hangs up, I run over to him and give him a big hug.

Finally, we upload the video to the internet. I ask my parents to share it online with the PTA, family, friends, neighbors, Ms. Cruz, and anyone else they can think of. We need to get the word out, and fast!

"I'm going to share with everyone I know!" I say, and I make sure my friends at school do too. Then, a couple of days later, something extraordinary happens. When I get to school, Auggie and Christina run up to me and both talk at once.

"You won't believe what's happening!" Auggie says.

"The video is everywhere!" Christina says, in the loudest voice I've ever heard her use.

"You've seen it?" I ask.

"In like three places," Auggie says. "My parents got it on the school listserv, and my abuelita called and said it was shared on her church's Facebook page. The teenager who lives next door to me showed it to me on his iPhone—someone had forwarded it him!"

"Our next-door neighbor stopped me when I was walking Wolf to say she's seen it and told

Sarai

me that she supports what we kids are doing!" Christina says. "My neighbor also said she forwarded the video to the mayor, who she knows personally."

"That's awesome!" I say. "Now maybe we'll get more people to come to our concert and donate to the music program!"

"Sarai," I hear a voice say, "I need to talk with you." I turn around, and it is Principal Harris. "Am I in trouble?"

"No." She smiles. "Quite the opposite. I just wanted you to know that a local news crew is

coming today to interview Ms. Cruz about our music program and the video you and the kids made."

"I don't understand," I say. "Why do they want to do a story about us?"

"Because," Auggie says, "we've been trying to tell you. You've gone viral! We've gone viral!"

"There's been so much interest in our music program thanks to the video that the local news has asked Ms. Cruz to come on to talk about it," says Principal Harris.

My head is spinning.

Later that afternoon, Ms. Cruz walks into our classroom.

"How did the interview go, Ms. Cruz?" Auggie asks.

"What's happening with the music program now?" I follow up.

"Are we going to be famous?" Valéria asks.

"Students!" Ms. Cruz says excitedly. "I have good news. The reporter told me that the superintendent of schools made a positive statement supporting the arts, so that's a good sign!" We all start cheering and clapping.

"Nothing final has been decided, so don't get too excited. And I hate to cut the celebration short," Ms. Cruz says, "but we need to practice. We need to be our best at the concert next Friday—the community is expecting us to make them proud!" We warm up with scales and then turn to our new song.

"I wanted to announce our two percussion soloists for the concert next Friday. It was a tough decision because you are all amazing. But this time, our soloists will be Auggie and . . . Ellie." My heart feels like it sinks into my stomach. I wanted a solo so bad. I think Ms. Cruz can tell I'm upset, because after class she says, "Sarai, can I talk to you for a minute?" I just nod my head. I'm afraid if I say something I'll cry. "I know you are disappointed about the solo, and I would be too. But Ellie and Auggie have been practicing more than you lately, so they are the best prepared for next week."

"But I've been busy trying to save the program!" I say.

"I know," Ms. Cruz says, "and I understand and appreciate you more than you can imagine. I realize that you've sacrificed lots of hours to help the program, so I thought you'd be the perfect person to introduce our Sparkles Sanchez song, along with the others we will be playing. You can be our emcee!"

"I would love to be the emcee!" I say, smiling. "I don't need to practice talking! I'm good at that."

"You're a good drummer too, Sarai," Ms. Cruz assures me. "It's just hard to do it all." I think about what Ms. Cruz says.

"If the music program gets saved, it will definitely be worth it," I say.

"You know what Sarai?" Ms. Cruz says. "Even if the music program DOESN'T get saved, I'll think it was all worth it."

I agree. But to be honest, I'm still kind of worried.

# CHAPTER 7

# THE BIG SHOW

It is the Friday night of the big concert, and I'm a little nervous. The gym at Martin Luther King Jr. Elementary is more packed than I've ever seen it, and it seems like our whole town is here. We have a table with a box for financial donations, and we have another table with a bunch of postcards addressed to the school district, the mayor, and the governor. Parents and kids can write out reasons why they hope the music program will

be saved, and Ms. Cruz has promised to drop them off at the post office early tomorrow.

I've done a lot of research about Sparkles Sanchez, and I'm excited to share what I've learned about her and the song we will be singing, "Glitter and Gleam." I've memorized my introduction. Usually, the fourth graders would go first, then the fifth and sixth graders, then the seventh graders, and the eighth graders in Advanced Band would go last. But today, because of all our efforts to save the program, Ms. Cruz decided that we, the fourth graders, are going to close the show. And what a show! Every single class does great. Finally, it's our turn. Ms. Cruz introduces us, and we play our first two songs. We get a big round of applause. It's time for our fantastic finale. I walk up to the microphone, take a deep breath, and

look at Ms. Cruz, who is standing offstage. She gives me a nod and two thumbs up.

"Thanks again, everyone, for coming!" I say loud and proud. "I represent Ms. Cruz's fourth-grade music class—level-one band. We are so happy to see everyone here, and we appreciate all of the support we've had from each of you! We have a special surprise for you tonight, parents, friends, and music lovers! We are going to end the night with a special song that we hope will put a sparkle in your eye. It's called 'Glitter and Gleam,' and it was written by Stefanie 'Sparkles' Sanchez, a girl who grew up less than fifteen miles from here, in the Bronx, and who first learned to play guitar in her elementary music class. I looked up the word 'gleam' in the dictionary and it means reflected light, and the fact that we have filled up this gym is a reflection of our love for music and the light it brings to each of us!" I say. Then I stop talking and look out at the audience. They start clapping.

"Do you want to save our music program?" I ask.

"Yes!" the audience responds, clapping.

"Are you sure?" I ask again.

"Yes!" the audience says, clapping and yelling a little louder.

"Do you want us to play 'Glitter and Gleam'?" I ask. All of a sudden, it seems like every single person in the entire gym jumps up and cheers at

the same time. Actually it's more like they scream. It sounds like a roar. I'm kind of in shock, but I guess they're *really* excited about our song.

"Turn around, Sarai!" I hear Auggie say from behind me, above the roar of the crowd. I turn around, and then I see her. Now I understand why the crowd is going crazy. Right behind me, smiling and waving to the crowd is . . .

"Sparkles Sanchez!" I yell, not realizing I'm still holding the microphone. She laughs and walks over and puts her hand on my shoulder. She has long pink fingernails with—what else?— sparkles on them. I'm in shock. I say the first thing I think of.

"You smell like flowers," I say, and then I hand her the microphone. She laughs and says, "Hi, Sarai."

Stefanie "Sparkles" Sanchez knows my name! She then takes my hand and turns to the audience. I can't quite believe this is happening. Sparkles Sanchez is here, standing next to me, at Martin Luther King Jr. Elementary. In our very own gym!

"Let's make some noise in support of music programs for kids!" Sparkles says. "Who wants a song?" The crowd is going crazy. Everyone has

their phones out, and there are so many flashes and pictures it seems like the gym is full of stars. Sparkles turns to us and asks, "Are you ready to sparkle and shine, musicians?"

"Yes!" we say, and I run over to my snare drum.

TAP

AP

"One, two," Sparkles says, tapping her foot, "ONE TWO THREE!" and then she starts singing. We play our hearts out and it feels like the whole community is singing along with her and us. At the end of the song, Sparkles shouts, "Shine bright! Reflect the light!" and then she disappears backstage, and just like that, she's gone.

"Did that really happen?" I ask Christina. "Or am I in a dream?"

"It was real," Christina says.

After the concert, I rush to find my family. I see my Tata and Mama Rosí first.

"Mi estrella!" Tata says. "You were truly a star tonight!"

"You were wonderful, Sarai!" Mama Rosí says. I hug them both.

Then all at once my other grandparents, Mama Chila and Papá, my parents, and my sisters find me. I'm hugged and kissed and congratulated.

"Glitter and gleam!" Mama Chila says, and does a little dance.

"Good job, Sarai!" Josie signs.

"Sparkles Sanchez is soooooooooo beautiful," Lucía says, jumping up and down.

"And such an amazing singer!" Mom says. "I took lots of pictures!"

"I'm proud of you, Sarai," Dad says. "Gonzalezes never give up!"

"No, they don't," I agree, hugging each member of my family. "I'm so happy you are here. This is the BEST night of my life so far," I say, and I mean it. "Did we raise enough money to save the program?" I ask my dad.

"I'm not sure," he says, "but Ms. Cruz did tell me that Sparkles Sanchez made her own special donation to the school district."

"Really?" I say. "That's amazing. How did she know about our concert?" I wonder.

"It must have been the video," Dad says.

"It must have been," I agree.

# CHAPTER 8

## CUPCAKES, FLOWERS, AND SURPRISES

I'm feeling so happy and grateful when I wake up on Saturday that I spend all morning baking. I want to do something nice for the world and the people in it. That afternoon, I walk over to Martínez and Sons to drop off some cupcakes for Mr. Martínez.

"Gracias, Sarai!" he says. Then I head over to the Washingtons' house with a dozen cupcakes— enough for their four hungry boys and a few of their friends too. Finally, I walk over to Señora

Sanchez's house, through her amazing garden, and up the steps to knock on her door.

"¡Buenas tardes!" I say when she answers. "I have a surprise for you. Your favorite triple-chocolate raspberry-cream cupcakes." I hand her the tray, and she smiles.

"Sarai, you've got to come in and have one with me," she says.

"Sure!" I say. I always like visiting Señora Sanchez's house. Everything is different shades of pink, and the inside even smells like flowers. Señora Sanchez doesn't have children, but she does have lots of nieces and nephews. I know this because her walls are covered with pictures.

While Señora Sanchez goes into the kitchen to get milk for me and café con leche for herself, I sit on her floral couch and look at the pictures along her back wall. I smile when I see a picture of a girl around my age wearing a pink shirt with turquoise glitter letters that spell out "Te amo," I love you. She has her arms wrapped around Señora Sanchez. There's something about her that looks familiar.

"Here you go, Sarai," Señora Sanchez says, walking back in with a cupcake on a plate. She hands me a tall glass of cold milk. She sips her café con leche and takes a bite of the cupcake I made her.

"These are so delicious!" she says. "Yum!"

"I'm so glad you like them," I say, still looking at the picture on the wall. What is it that it reminds me of? Then, all of a sudden, it hits me. I jump up and walk over to the picture of Señora Sanchez and the little girl. I look more closely. In the right-hand corner, it says:

*To my favorite Tía, with lots of Love, Stefanie* ♥

"That's Stefanie 'Sparkles' Sanchez!" I say. "It was you! You sent her the video! You're a Sanchez too. You're her aunt!"

"Take a breath, sweetie," Señora Sanchez says, laughing. "I wondered if you would ever figure it out. Stefanie is my great-niece on my brother's side. I used to babysit her and her brother when they were little, before I moved out here to the suburbs."

"So YOU helped save the music program," I say, still shocked. "Why didn't you ever mention that you were related to Sparkles Sanchez?"

"People get a little crazy about famous people. So I'm going to ask you not to mention it to anyone else in the neighborhood," she says.

"Not even my parents?" I say. "I tell them everything."

"As you should," Señora Sanchez says, smiling. "But . . ."

"But what?" I ask.

"They already know," Señora Sanchez says, laughing again at the look on my face.

When I get home, I run up the front steps and find my family in the living room.

"Mom! Dad!" I say. "I can't believe you didn't tell me about Señora Sanchez."

"What about Señora Sanchez?" Lucía asks. Mom raises her eyebrows at me, and Dad gives me a look.

"You didn't tell me that she helped the music program too," I say, realizing that the last person on earth who can keep a secret is my littlest sister.

"Well, she did," Dad says. "In fact, Ms. Cruz called while you were out, and we raised enough funding to cover the program for another two years!"

"And," Mom says, "Ms. Cruz thinks that we've gotten so much attention that no one will dare to get rid of our program for a long time."

"Wow," I say. "That's awesome. This is inspiring. I'm going to go practice on my drum pad. I have an idea for a song!"

"Your own song?" Josie signs.

"Yes!" I say. "I have a message to share."

"Well?" Lucía asks. "What is it?"

"SPREAD THE SPARKLE!" I say, and everyone laughs.

LOOK OUT

FOR MORE

# AWESOME ADVENTURES

WITH SARAI